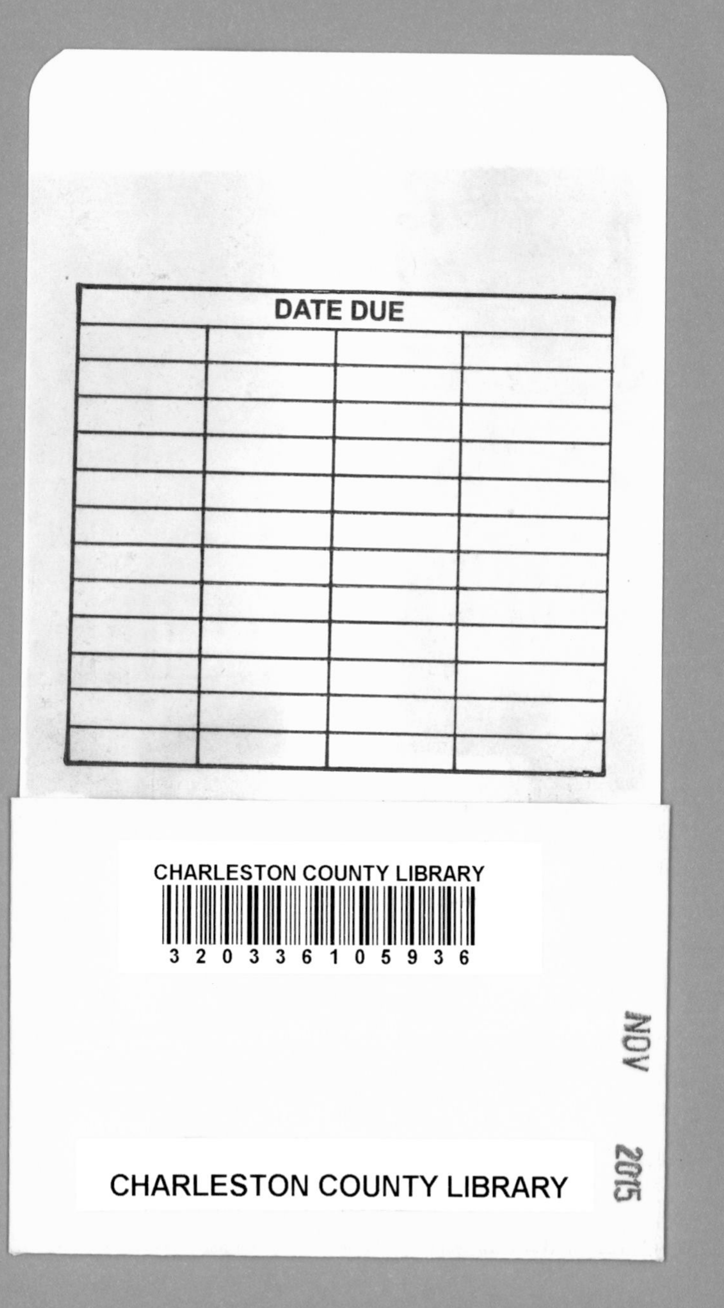

• Alyssa Satin Capucilli •

Tulip and Rex Write a Story

• Illustrated by Sarah Massini •

Katherine Tegen Books
An Imprint of HarperCollinsPublishers

Katherine Tegen Books is an imprint of HarperCollins Publishers.

Tulip and Rex Write a Story

www.harpercollinschildrens.com

ISBN 978-0-06-209416-2

The artist used mixed traditional media and Photoshop to create the digital illustrations for this book.
Typography by Martha Rago
15 16 17 18 19 SCP 10 9 8 7 6 5 4 3 2 1
❖
First Edition

For Edward Schecter, who always finds the perfect story

—A.S.C.

For Martha and Katie

—S.M.

One beautiful spring morning, Tulip leaped out of bed with a hop and a spin. Tulip loved to dance.

Rex wagged his tail and spun about in a circle. He loved to dance, too.

“What would you like to do today, Rex?” asked Tulip. “We could read our storybook, or play pretend . . .”

Rex scratched his ear. Those both sounded fun!

Tulip had started digging in her dress-up box when the doorbell rang!

"It's a package
from Grandma, Rex.
It's a notebook!"

Rex barked. He found something in the box, too. It was a new leash!

“That’s a great idea, Rex!” said Tulip. “We’ll go for a walk.”

Tulip and Rex galloped outside into the morning sun.

They skipped cheerfully down the street. Rex sniffed around and wagged his tail!

"It's a polka-dotted ladybug, Rex. Polka dots make me want to *hop*."

Tulip hopped up and down and up and down. Hopping was hard for Rex. Still, he did his very best.

THE RITZ
DANCE STUDIO

"H-O-P

is such a happy word," said Tulip.

Rex scratched at Tulip's notebook.

"That's another great idea, Rex! We'll find more wonderful words like *hop* and tuck them into the notebook."

"It's a whole new way of taking a walk!" said Tulip.

Rex rolled from side to side! A word walk *was* a great idea!

Just then, a butterfly landed atop Rex's nose!
"Butterflies flutter, Rex. Flutter, flutter.

Flutter

is a lovely word,
don't you think?"

Rex wagged his tail. *Flutter* *was* a lovely word; it tickled, too! Into the notebook it went!

And butterfly, too.

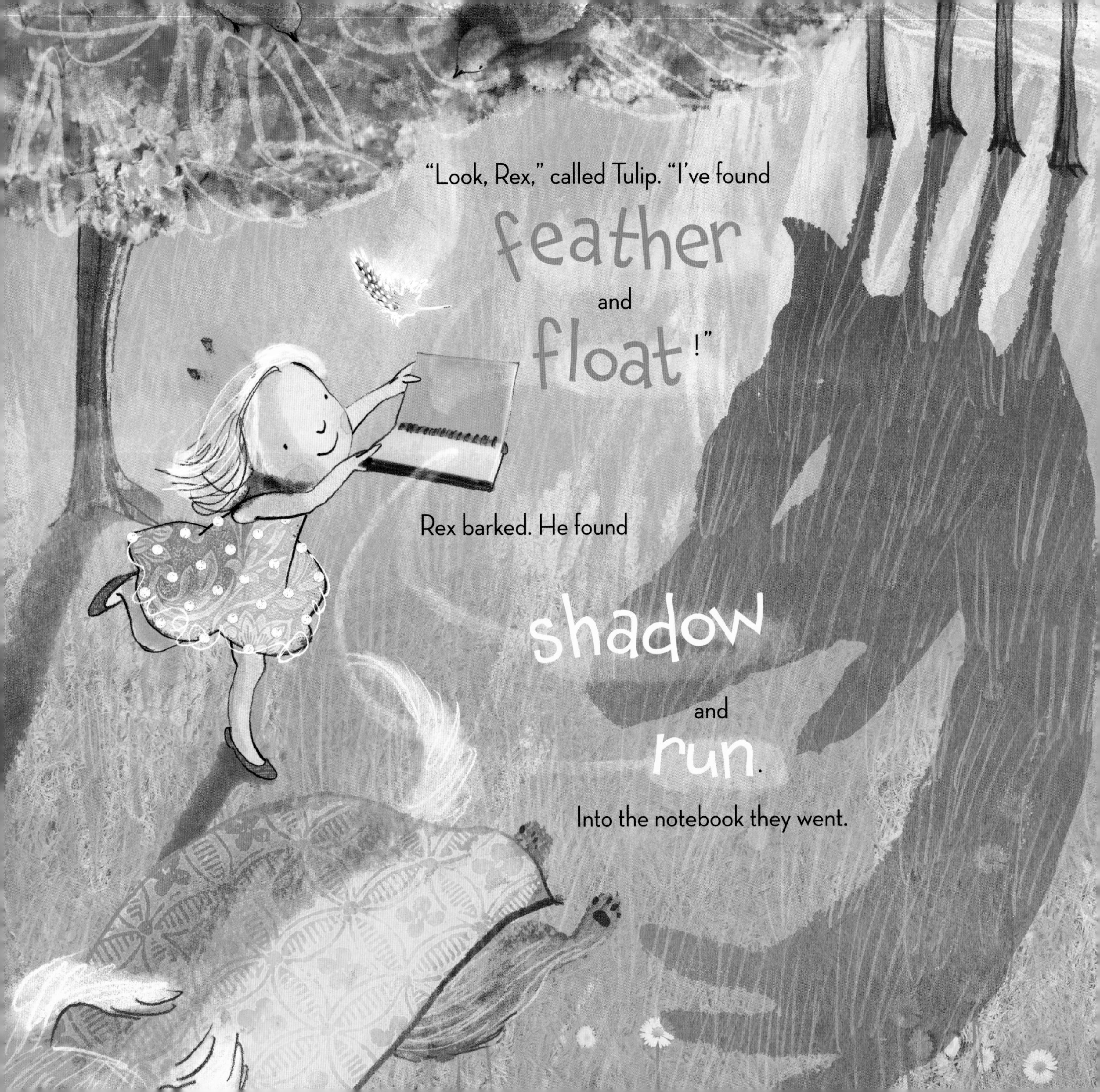

"Look, Rex," called Tulip. "I've found

feather

and

float!"

Rex barked. He found

shadow

and

run.

Into the notebook they went.

"Over here, Rex," called Tulip. "I'm sure there are more words on the other side!"

Tulip bent down low. She held her head high. And then, Tulip leaped!

SPLASH!

Tulip landed in the small stream. Their notebook did, too.

Rex barked. He wagged his tail. He reached his paw down, down, down and helped a somewhat soggy Tulip, and the notebook, out of the stream.

Tulip buried her face in Rex's soft, soft ears.

"You may not be quite like other dogs, Rex, but I'm sure you are the *bravest* and *kindest* dog in the world," said Tulip.

"Brave and kind are two very special words for our notebook. Don't you think so, Rex?"

Rex lifted his paw and gave a huge stretch!

"Rex!" said Tulip. "You look just like the king from our storybook."

Now Tulip stretched up high.
"That gives me an idea!" she said.

Tulip eagerly flipped through the pages of the notebook.

Rex sat right by her side.

"I've got it, Rex!" Tulip said with a hop. "Are you ready?"

Rex wagged his tail!

"Once upon a time," Tulip began . . .

"... there was a *brave* and *kind* king named Rex and his queen, Tulip. They loved to dance!"

"One day, a fierce dragon captured Queen Tulip from the castle. King Rex galloped through the forest until at last he found Queen Tulip balancing at the edge of a deep, wide moat. Queen Tulip wobbled back and forth and back and forth. The ***shadow*** of the dragon loomed overhead. Could King Rex save his queen?

"King Rex reached down, down, down toward Queen Tulip. Queen Tulip stretched on her tiptoes toward King Rex. Alas, she was just out of his reach.

"But wait! There came a ***feather floating*** from the sky. It was no ordinary feather; why, it seemed to dance! King Rex grasped the magical feather and held it aloft and, as if he had the wings of a ***butterfly***, King Rex sailed across the moat and—"

"It's time for lunch, Tulip and Rex!" Tulip's parents called.

"To be continued, Rex," said Tulip, hugging the notebook with a cheerful skip. "Who knows what will happen next? Still, I'm sure there will be many more words and stories to come for this king and queen."

Rex barked.
He wagged his tail.
He could hardly wait!